O9-ABI-912

DISCARD

I'm Deaf and It's Okay

Lorraine Aseltine
Evelyn Mueller
Nancy Tait

pictures by Helen Cogancherry

Albert Whitman & Company, Niles, Illinois

Library of Congress Cataloging-in-Publication Data

Aseltine, Lorraine.
I'm deaf, and it's okay.

Summary: A young boy describes the frustrations caused by his deafness and the encouragement he receives from a deaf teenager that he can lead an active life.
I. Children, Deaf—Juvenile literature. [1.Deaf. 2. Physically handicapped] I. Mueller, Evelyn. II. Tait, Nancy. III. Cogancherry, Helen, ill. IV. Title.
HV2392.A84 1986 362.4'2'088054 85-26446
ISBN 0-8075-3472-2

The text of this book is set in fourteen-point Baskerville.

Published in 1986 by Albert Whitman & Company, Niles, Illinois
Published simultaneously in Canada by General Publishing, Limited, Toronto

10 9 8 7 6 5 4 3

This book is dedicated to
all small boys and girls who wear hearing aids
L.A. E.M. N.T

To Herb H.C.

It is nighttime.
It is very dark in my bedroom,
and I am in bed, without my hearing aids.
I can't see much,
and I can't hear anything.
Maybe that shadow in the corner is a monster!
I feel alone.
I am afraid.
I start to cry.

Mom comes right away and turns on the light.
I feel better when she holds me.
She signs and talks to me about how dark it seems
when my hearing aids are on the night table,
instead of in my ears.
I can't hear Mom at all,
but I understand what she says.
I watch her lips and hands as she signs to me.
I put my hand on her throat and feel
her voice purring as she speaks.
She helps me snuggle down into my soft bed,
and she kisses me.

I feel safe and warm.
In a little while, I start to fall asleep.

On Saturday Molly and I play dress-up.
We put on grown-up clothes.
Even with my hearing aids in,
I can't hear much that Molly says.
But she knows how to sign, and I watch her lips.
We have fun.

Suddenly Molly is gone. I look around.
"Molly, where are you?" I say.

Oh, I see Molly. She's talking on the telephone.
I didn't hear it ring.
"Who is it?" I ask. "Who are you talking to?
Is it Dad? Grandma? Tell me!"

Molly doesn't pay any attention to me.
I feel sad and left out.
I wish I could talk on the phone like Molly can.
But I can't hear well enough.
I need to see someone's lips
to understand what the person is saying.

Monday is one of my favorite days at school.
My class goes to the library for story hour.
Our librarian speaks into a microphone
and uses sign language to tell a story.
The microphone and my big school hearing aid
help me hear some of her words.
I hear her better than if
I was just wearing my regular hearing aids.
I listen very hard and watch her.
I like the story.

But wait a minute!
All of a sudden I can't hear anything.
Maybe something is wrong with my school hearing aid.

I raise my hand and tell the librarian
I have to go back to my classroom.

BIG

It's a long way back,
but I go by myself.
I tell my teacher I can't hear
and that maybe something is wrong
with my school hearing aid.
She checks it. "Yes," she says, "you're right.
You need a new cord. That was good thinking."

I feel proud of myself.
My teacher changes the cord,
and I hurry back to the library.
I want to hear the rest of the story.

After school I see my friends in the neighborhood,
looking at some pictures.
They are talking and laughing.

I want to see the pictures, too.

Now they have stopped talking and laughing.
What happened?
Were they talking about me?
Don't they like me anymore?
Did I do something wrong?

My friend Tom shows me the pictures.
He doesn't know how to sign,
but he remembers to look at me when he talks.
I watch his lips, and my hearing aids help me
understand some of the words he says.
Tom says, "We are talking about Halloween.
What are you going to wear?"

Oh, Halloween!
They are talking about Halloween,
not about me.
I feel better.
I think I will be a clown on Halloween.

I'm happy when Grandma comes to visit us.
She brings a new book for Molly and me.
I want to show Grandma the painting
I made for her.

Where is Grandma?
Oh, she's in the big chair with Molly,
reading her the new book.
Grandma is talking about the pictures,
and Molly is laughing.
I want Grandma to talk to me like that!
I think Grandma likes Molly better than me
because Molly can hear and talk better than I can.
I feel angry!
I hate Molly!

I push her on the floor.
I climb into Grandma's lap myself.
Now Molly is crying, and Grandma is angry at me!
She says it is wrong to hurt my little sister.
Why doesn't she understand?

Dad and I talk to Grandma.
Dad helps Grandma understand that
sometimes I feel left out.
I tell Molly I'm sorry I pushed her.
I really don't hate her—I was just mad.

Grandma says she loves both me and Molly a lot.
She hugs me hard.
I love Grandma a lot, too,
and I feel better now.

Sometimes I go shopping with Mom.
Today we are in a big department store.
Mom says, "Hurry—we don't have much time."
I stop to look at a neat football.
I want to show it to Mom. "Look, Mom!" I say.

But when I turn around, I don't see her.
I'm afraid and mixed-up.
I don't know which way to go.
I try to tell a lady that I lost my mom.
The lady doesn't understand me—
I can tell by the funny look on her face.
I tell her again. She still doesn't understand.
She isn't used to my voice
the way my family and friends are.
Maybe no one will help me!
What will I do if I can't find my mom?

I am really scared now,
but I remember to stay in one place,
like Mom told me to do if I ever got lost.

PUPPETS
5.49
Special

Here comes Mom!
She is hurrying, and she looks worried.
We both laugh, and we hug each other.
She says she was afraid, too,
but she is proud of me
for staying in one place and being brave.

TOYS GALORE
BALLS
MINI-MOUSE
2.95

Some people make weird faces when they talk to me.
They stretch their mouths wide and speak very loudly.
I wonder why they do that.
Do they think I'm stupid?

Dad tells me that people think I can read their lips better
when they stretch their mouths wide and talk loud.
They don't know very loud voices bother me.
They don't know I like it best when
people don't yell and look right at me when they talk.

I think I will like it when I am grown-up
because then I won't need my hearing aids any more.
None of the big people I know wear hearing aids.
I will hear Mom's voice and Dad's voice and Molly's voice.
I will hear the night sounds.
I will hear what my friends are saying.
I will hear what the teacher is saying.
People won't stretch their mouths
and shout when they talk to me.
I won't feel left out.
I will talk, and people will understand what I say.
I will be just like everyone else.

Mom and Dad say this won't happen.
They say I will always need my hearing aids to help me hear.
They say it will be okay to be grown-up
and wear hearing aids.

I feel mad!
I don't want to wear hearing aids when I'm grown-up.
I don't want to at all!

As soon as I get to school the next day,
I ask my teacher if I will have to
wear hearing aids when I grow up.
She says I will.
She says she understands how I feel.
I shout, "How do you know how I feel?
You don't wear hearing aids!"

I pull my hearing aids out of my ears
and throw them on the floor.

My teacher makes me pick them up.
She watches me while I put my hearing aids on again.
We talk about my angry feelings,
but I still feel mad.

Picture
10 strong

Today Brian is visiting our classroom.
He is seventeen, and he wears hearing aids,
just like me and the other children in my class.
Brian says, "It's okay to be grown-up
and wear hearing aids.
Really, it is."
I say, "NO. It's *not* okay!"

Brian smiles and says he felt the same way
when he was a little boy.
Brian says that deaf people can do most things
that hearing people do.
He drives a car, takes karate lessons,
and has lots of friends.
After school he has a part-time job,
and next year he's going to college.

Brian goes with us on our field trip to the zoo.
At the zoo there's lots to see and touch.
I like watching the lions stretch and yawn on the rocks.
I like to feel the rough skin of the elephant's ear.

The children's zoo is the best.
The lady takes out a big snake,
and everyone gets to touch it.
It feels cold and dry.

Then we pass around a baby rabbit.
Brian gives the rabbit to me.
It wiggles its nose and blinks its eyes.
Brian wiggles his nose, too, and winks at me.

HANDLE
TH CARE

On the bus going home, I sit next to Brian.
He lets me wear his new watch.
He talks about what he wants to study in college.
He wants to be a teacher.
Then he tells me the names
of all the cars that drive past the bus.
We are friends.

I feel good inside.
I think maybe it will be okay to be grown-up
and wear hearing aids.
Maybe I will be like Brian.
Maybe I will help a little deaf friend, too.

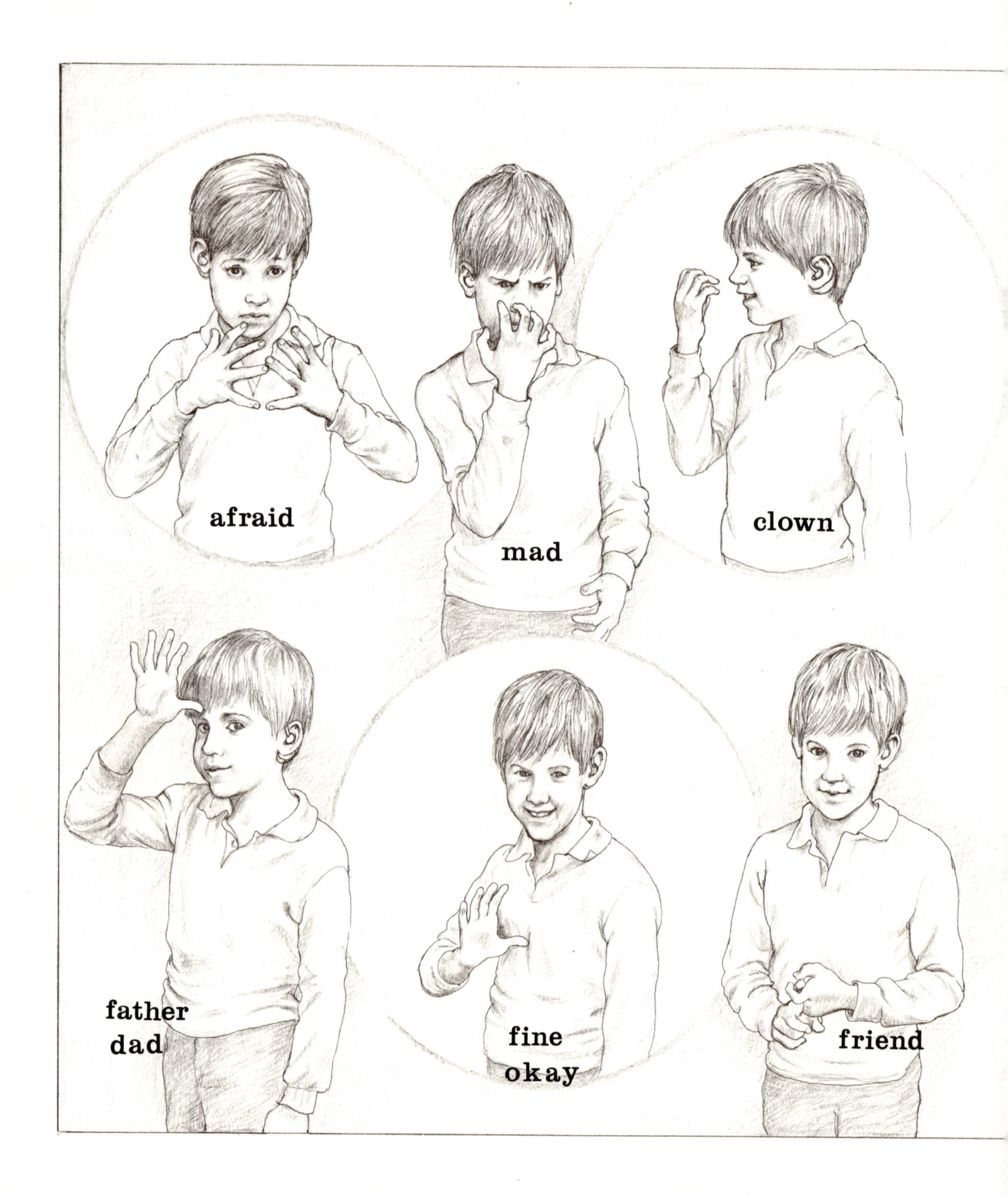
afraid
mad
clown
father
dad
fine
okay
friend

left out
love
mixed-up
mother
mom
sad
talk

LORRAINE ASELTINE has a master's degree in deaf education and has worked with hearing-impaired preschool children at Hammerschmidt School and Pleasant Lane School in Lombard, Illinois, for over seventeen years. She believes it is important to nurture the whole child as well as to work with his or her disability. To help minimize the emotional problems deaf children so often have, she encourages her students to communicate their feelings and to develop positive self-images.

EVELYN MUELLER has a master's degree in speech and hearing science and has worked as a speech/language therapist at Pleasant Lane School for six years. There she helps hearing-impaired children communicate meaningfully and expand their speech, language, and auditory skills, no matter what their hearing loss.

NANCY TAIT is the mother of a deaf young adult and has worked as an aide in the preschool hearing-impaired classroom at Pleasant Lane School. As a parent, she has special understanding of the emotional needs and language problems of hearing-impaired children and the importance of providing them with positive role models within the hearing-impaired community.